No Milk!

Jennifer A. Ericsson pictures by Ora Eitan

TAMBOURINE BOOKS  NEW YORK

Text copyright © 1993 by Jennifer A. Ericsson
Illustrations copyright © 1993 by Ora Eitan

The illustrations were created with gouache and pastel on paper.

Library of Congress Cataloging in Publication Data

Ericsson, Jennifer A. No milk!/by Jennifer A. Ericsson:
pictures by Ora Eitan.—1st ed. p. cm.
Summary: A city boy has a great deal of trouble coaxing milk out of a dairy cow.
[1. Cows —Fiction. 2. Milking—Fiction.] I. Eitan, Ora, 1940-ill. II. Title.
PZ7.E72584No 1993 [E]—dc20 92-21806 CIP AC
ISBN 0-688-11306-0.—ISBN 0-688-11307-9 (lib. bdg.)
10 9 8 7 6 5 4 3 2 1
First edition

To Beth, who has shared my dreams since childhood

J.A.E.

To my parents

O.E.

 A dairy cow.

 A city boy.

 A silver pail.

 A wooden stool.

But no milk!

A pat on the head.
A scratch on the ear.
A kiss on the nose
From the city boy.

But no milk!

Some friendly words.
A handful of grass.
A bucket of grain.
A bundle of hay.

But no milk!

A funny joke
Gets a good laugh
From the duck, the horse,
The chickens and sheep.

But no milk!

A little song.
A little dance.
A great big bow
From the city boy.

But no milk!

The city boy
Picks up some eggs.
He juggles them high,
And drops not a one.

But no milk!

A handstand.
A cartwheel.
A somersault.
Some magic tricks.

But no milk!

An angry frown.
A shaking fist.
Two stomping feet.
A screaming boy.

But no milk!

The cow kicks.
The pail flies.
The animals hide.
The boy cries.

But no milk!

The city boy
Finds the dented pail.
He sits back down
On the wooden stool.

But no milk!

He rests his head
Upon the cow.
He gently touches
Her swollen udder.

But no milk!

A little pat?
A little squeeze?
A little tug?
Could it be?

Milk!

A great big smile
On a city boy.
A great big lick
From a happy cow.
And lots of milk!